THE SANDCASTLE

M. P. Robertson

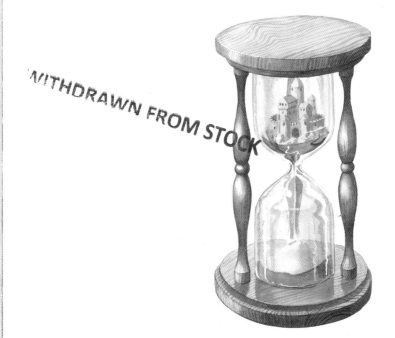

FRANCES LINCOLN

There was nothing in the whole world that Jack liked better than building sandcastles. But as strong as he built the walls and as high as he built the towers, he couldn't stop the sea from stealing them away.

For Sophy

British Library Cataloguing in Publication Data available on request

ISBN 0-7112-1732-7

Printed in Singapore
1 3 5 7 9 8 6 4 2

At the end of a perfect day, Jack looked proudly at his latest sandcastle. As the tide rolled in, he stood stubbornly in its path.

"Stay back, sea!" he ordered. "This is my castle; I'm king here."

But the sea just spat at his knees.

Then something caught Jack's eye – a shell that glistened like a jewel. He placed it on the highest turret of his sandcastle, then shut his eyes tight.

"I wish my sandcastle was as big as a real castle and I wish that I was king," he said.

But when he opened his eyes, his castle hadn't grown an inch and he was still just a boy on a beach.

That evening Jack was woken by the squabbling of the gulls. He drew back the curtains and rubbed his eyes in disbelief.

His first wish had come true.

Jack sneaked down to the beach, and as he
drew near to the castle the drawbridge lowered.
Jack wasn't scared. This was his castle, so he
marched across.

He was met at the gatehouse by a girl whose eyes
were as blue as the ocean.

"We've been waiting for you," she said. Then,
placing a shell to her lips, she blew a salty note.

At her signal the doors to a great hall swung open. Jack was greeted by a fanfare of trumpets, and was led through a cheering crowd to a seashell throne. The girl placed a pearly crown on his head.

"Hail, King Jack!" cheered the crowd. "The king of the sandcastle."

His second wish had come true.

A band struck up a tune and the girl led Jack into a merry jig. Through the night they danced. In the frenzy, no one heard the waves slapping against the great doors.

At last, the doors could no longer
hold back the sea. With a thunderous crash
they gave way. The ocean roared in, sweeping
people off their dancing feet.

As the water washed over the crowd they
began to change! Jack watched in amazement as
their feet became tails and their skin became scales.

The girl dragged Jack up a staircase away from the rising
water. From the battlements he watched in horror as the
waves bit chunks from his sandcastle.

"Stay back, sea!" he ordered. "I'm a real king now!
Look, I've got a crown."

"You may be a king," said the girl,
"but even a king can't stop the sea."

The water continued to rise. They ran up the inside of a tower. Higher and higher they went but the sea was always just one step behind, lapping at their heels.

When Jack reached the top of the tower he heard the girl say, "Good luck, Jack. And don't forget your fairytales. You always get three wishes."

Jack looked around but the girl had vanished. All he saw was the flash of a tail disappearing into the water.

Still the sea was rising. Jack scrambled on to
the turret. He found the shell that he had placed
there the day before, only now it was as big as
a boat. He heaved it into the water and climbed in.

As the sea swallowed the last of his castle,
Jack clung tightly to the shell.

"I don't want to be a king any more," he said.
"I wish I was safe at home in bed."

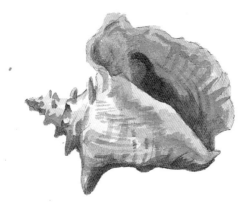

Far in the distance there came a long, salty note.
Then, the shell was lifted high on the crest of
a wave and swept back to the shore.

When Jack awoke he was no longer on the beach but wrapped warmly in his duvet. Beside him on the pillow lay the magic shell.

He jumped out of bed and hurried down to the beach. The sea had polished it as smooth as a mirror.

As a new sandcastle began to take shape, Jack felt very happy. Being a king was all very well, but there was nothing he liked better in the whole world than being a boy, on a beach, building sandcastles.

And as the tide turned and licked at the walls of his castle, he just smiled.